Oil Paints

by Mari Bolte   illustrated by Pamela Becker

Content Consultant:
Robert A. Williams
Artist and Teacher
Instructor of Commercial and Technical Art
South Central College, North Mankato, Minnesota

CAPSTONE PRESS
a capstone imprint

Snap Books are published by Capstone Press,
1710 Roe Crest Drive, North Mankato, Minnesota 56003.
www.capstonepub.com

Copyright © 2014 by Capstone Press, a Capstone imprint.
All rights reserved.

No part of this publication may be reproduced
in whole or in part, or stored in a retrieval system,
or transmitted in any form or by any means,
electronic, mechanical, photocopying, recording,
or otherwise, without written permission of the publisher.
For information regarding permission, write to Capstone Press,
1710 Roe Crest Drive, North Mankato, Minnesota 56003.

Library of Congress Cataloging-in-Publication Data
Bolte, Mari.
  Oil paints / By Mari Bolte ; illustrated by Pamela Becker.
    pages cm. — (Snap books. Paint it)
  Summary: "Step-by-step guides show how to create a variety of projects using oil paints"—Provided by publisher.
  ISBN 978-1-4765-3110-6 (library binding)
  ISBN 978-1-4765-3568-5 (ebook PDF)
 1. Painting—Technique—Juvenile literature. I. Becker, Pamela. II. Title.
  ND1146.B645 2014
  751.45—dc23   2013005394

Designer: Bobbie Nuytten
Production Specialist: Laura Manthe

Photo Credits:
Illustrations by Pamela Becker; All photos by Capstone Studio and Pamela Becker except the following: Newscom: Joseph Martin, 14 (bottom left), 21 (bottom left), 29 (bottom left)

Printed in the United States of America in
Stevens Point, Wisconsin.
032013   007227WZF13

Table of Contents

In Your Art Box 4
Transparent and Opaque 8
Tiny Art.. 10
Impasto Owl 13
Indirect Sushi 16
Direct Sushi................................... 18
Seurat Dots 20
Picasso's Pets................................ 22
Plein Air 25
In the Style Of 28

Read More 32
Internet Sites................................. 32

IN YOUR ART BOX

Load your brush and get familiar with the most classic of paints. Oil paints were first used in the 1300s. They became widely used in Europe in the 1500s. Artists liked that the paint could be thickly applied or used to add tiny detail. They also can stand the test of time.

OIL PAINTS

Oil paints are made with dry pigments blended with an oil, usually linseed oil. Because it takes the oil so long to dry, oil paint is ideal for long projects.

Oil paints can also be blended to create realistic color combinations. The slow drying time allows the artist to create natural blends with many layers.

Paints and Pigments

All paints are made up of a pigment and a binder. Pigments are dry, colored powders. They can be natural or artificial. They can come from plants, animals, the earth, or a lab. Pigment is what colors all painting mediums. The only difference between paint mediums is the binder that is used.

Binders are adhesive liquids that hold pigment. Pigment reacts differently depending on the binder that is used. This is why one color of oil paint looks different than the same color of watercolor paint.

SURFACES

Because oil paints stay wet so long, they can rot or corrode painted surfaces. Canvases must be sealed to prevent the canvas from absorbing the oil. Untreated canvas will also cause your oil paints to appear dull. Canvas can be bought treated and untreated.

Wood panels, masonite boards, and pads of canvas paper can also be used.

BRUSHES AND KNIVES

Natural hair brushes are best for oil painting. They hold up well to oil paints and retain their shape. Brushes are usually made from the fur from members of the weasel family. Minks, kolinskies, and ermine are common. Squirrel, ox, goat, and skunk hair brushes are also used.

Brushes used for oil painting need to be cleaned after each use. Solvents such as turpentine or mineral spirits are traditionally used. Although they can be dangerous, some artists feel they are best at removing paint from brush bristles. Walnut or linseed oil, baby oil, or special brush soaps are safer, solvent-free choices. Wash brushes with mild soap and water before putting them away.

Knives and spatulas are helpful tools for any painter. Painting knives are used to apply paint. Palette knives are used to scrape paint and clean palettes. Spatulas can be used to mix paint and apply paint to the canvas.

Painting knives should be made of steel. The blades should not be too sharp. Sharp edges can cut into paint, canvas—and you. Edges can be dulled with sandpaper before use.

Steel painting knives shouldn't rust when used with oil paint.

TIPS AND TECHNIQUES

~ Keep your palette organized. Try to place every color on the same spot on your palette each time. Eventually you'll remember where red is, instead of having to look every time.

~ Oil crayons or pastels are other forms of oil paint. They are soft, pigmented sticks of wax and oil. Like oil paints, they can be built up in layers. They can also be thinned with mineral spirits and brushed on.

~ Use the basic technique of fat over lean when using oil paints. Lean paint has been thinned or diluted. Fat paint has more oil. Lean paint dries faster. If you paint lean over fat, the paint may not stick. It may also dry unevenly, which causes cracks in your painting. So start with lean paint for your underpainting. Then build as you go.

~ To keep your hands clean, wear latex gloves while painting and during cleanup. You can also use special barrier cream or shea butter. These will help protect you from toxic pigments.

~ For further protection, thin paints with walnut or linseed oil, rather than turpentine. If you do use turpentine, be sure to dispose of it properly. Seal it well and take it to your local recycling center.

~ To save paint for future uses, cover your palette tightly with plastic wrap. Then put it in the freezer. Discard any paint that has developed a "skin."

paint applied with palette knife; thinned paint applied with toothbrush

oil pastels

thickly-applied paint

layered paint

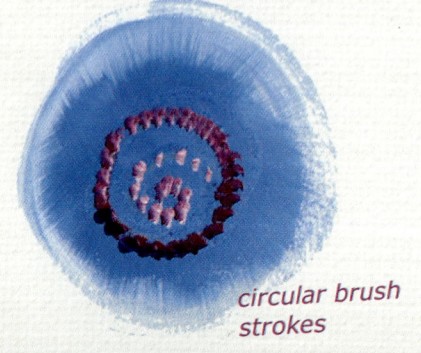

blended colors

circular brush strokes

wet brush onto dry paper

SEALING AND TONING

Applying gesso is an important step when using untreated canvas. Gesso is an acrylic sealer. It prevents oil from sinking into the canvas. It also gives the paint something to grab onto. Apply gesso to the canvas with a brush. Let it dry. Repeat steps to add a second and third layer.

Toning canvas is not always necessary. However, it gives your painting a base. It also helps the dark and light colors show up better.

First choose the color to tone your canvas. The toning paint should be a contrasting color to your finished project. Apply with a paintbrush or a piece of cheesecloth.

COLOR PALETTE

Oil paints come in many premixed colors. However, most artists start with a base palette of between eight and 12 main colors. Below is a list containing some of the more common colors:

Flake White, Cadmium Yellow, Cadmium Red, Permanent Rose, Permanent Alizarin Crimson, French Ultramarine, Cobalt Blue, Ultramarine, Prussian Blue, Raw Umber, Yellow Ochre, Burnt Sienna, Titanium White, Lamp Black

Some pigments are toxic. If you're not sure whether a pigment is toxic, check the label. Many toxic pigments have a metal in their name. Look for paints with barium, cadmium, cobalt, zinc, lead, chrome, and manganese.

Transparent and Opaque

Paint comes in transparent and opaque. Transparent paint allows light through. Opaque paint does not. Start your painting with opaque paint. Then add details and shadows with transparent layers.

Compare how transparent and opaque paints behave when applied in layers. The base layer disappears under the opaque paint. The base is always visible under the transparent paint.

opaque

opaque dark base

opaque magenta

opaque yellow

opaque magenta

applied over dark base

applied over magenta

applied over yellow

transparent

transparent dark base

transparent magenta

transparent yellow

transparent magenta

8

1. Sketch out your solar system. Use a compass to draw planets.

2. Mix a transparent blue for the sky. Paint the background and around the circles. Don't worry about being perfect—the planets will be painted with opaque paint, so any mistakes will be covered. Let dry completely.

3. To add stars, grab an old toothbrush. Thin white paint with gel medium. Dip the toothbrush bristles into the paint. Gently tap the head of the toothbrush over your painting. This will spatter white stars across the sky.

4. Paint the planets with a variety of opaque paints. Let this layer dry completely.

5. Add land and oceans to your planets with transparent paint. Experiment by layering many different colors over the base coat.

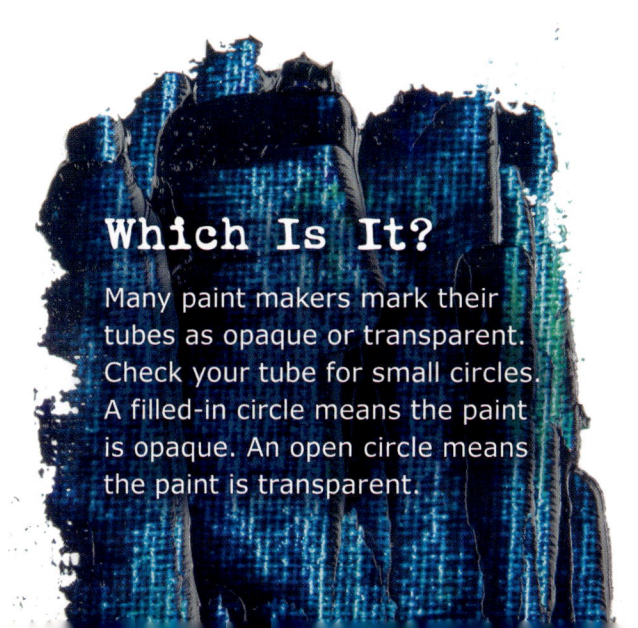

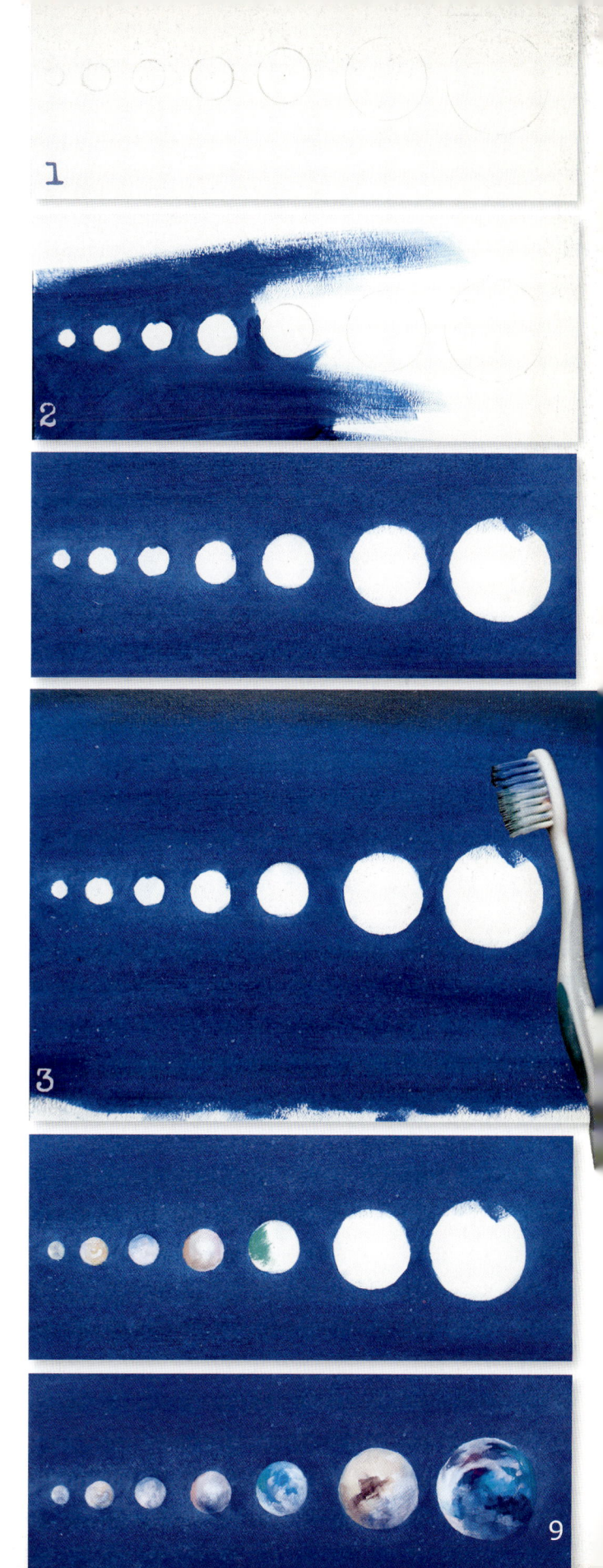

Which Is It?

Many paint makers mark their tubes as opaque or transparent. Check your tube for small circles. A filled-in circle means the paint is opaque. An open circle means the paint is transparent.

Tiny Art

Drawing thumbnails helps you plan ahead. You can decide what part of the painting will be the central focus. They also help you figure out the light and dark shades of the painting, called values.

Once you have a thumbnail sketch, you can turn it into a miniature painting. Painting in miniature allows you to work out any problem areas before starting your full-sized masterpiece.

1. Sketch your rough design onto tracing paper. Draw in light and shaded areas.

2. Draw a grid on the tracing paper and over the rough design.

3. Draw a grid onto another piece of paper. Use this paper for your miniature painting.

4. Copy the tracing paper grid square by square onto the new grid. Keep this drawing clean; do not add light and shadows. You will paint those in later.

5. Once your miniature sketch is complete, prepare your palette. Mix darks and lights of contrasting hues.

6. Identify your darkest and lightest areas first. Block these areas with paint. Pay more attention to the tones and contrast, rather than detail work.

7. Add the medium blocks of color to bring your miniature painting together.

8. Add any details you may have missed.

continued on next page

11

Another Angle

If your first thumbnail didn't turn out the way you wanted, try another! There are many ways to approach art. Switch up the painting's focus, tones, and values. This variation has a layer of light opaque paint added first. This layer will show through as you paint over it. Small changes can create a completely different piece of art.

1. Create a sketch and transfer it using the grid technique.
2. Lay a base layer of light opaque paint anywhere you want to represent natural light.
3. Add increasingly dark colors over the base layer. This will build contrast with your color values.

Impasto Owl

Impasto painting is the thick application of paint directly onto the canvas. Paintings with this technique can have an almost three-dimensional look.

continued on next page

1. Pencil the shape of the owl onto the canvas.

2. Use a brush to roughly paint the background. Flat bristled brushes work best for this.

The Starry Night

The Starry Night is one of the most well-known impasto paintings. It was done by Dutch artist Vincent Van Gogh (1853–1890). He painted it in 1889. He finished it in just three days. See also Impressionism (1874–1886) and Expressionism (early 1900s–1925).

Load paint onto your palette knife, or mix directly onto the canvas. For interesting color blends, load several colors onto the knife at once.

3. Use a palette knife to outline the owl's facial feathers. Squeeze paint directly from the tube and onto the palette knife.

4. Overlap with inner layers. Continue overlapping to build texture. Clean your palette knife in between colors.

5. Work from the middle of the painting toward the edges.

Paint applied too thickly may crack as it dries, so take care not to add too many layers.

To add extra texture, mix sand or sawdust with your paint. An impasto medium can be used to thicken oil paints too.

Indirect Sushi

Indirect painting is the traditional technique used with oil paints. Artists begin with an underpainting called grisaille, or gray painting. Underpainting establishes a painting's dark and light tones. Then regular paint is applied with glazes and scumbles. Because indirect painting requires underlayers to be dry, it is not for the impatient!

Glazes and Scumbles

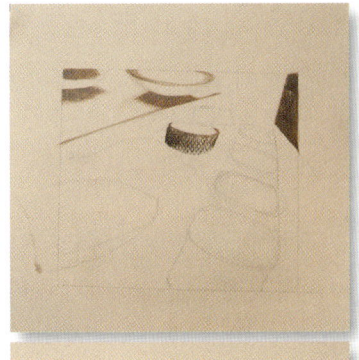

A **glaze** is a transparent layer of dark paint over light opaque paint. The opaque paint must be completely dry before applying the transparent layer. The transparent paint must be thinned. Glazes give paintings an appearance of depth.

A **scumble** is a layer of light paint applied over darker paint. Like glazing, the dark paint should be completely dry. However, it is not thinned. Scumbling is a great way to add light to your painting.

1. Lightly sketch your drawing onto paper. Choose colored paper that's not too light or too dark. This will make it easier to build the painting's values (light and dark parts) as you go.

2. Start with the grisaille layer. Mix black and white or Burnt Umber and white. See how many different grays you can create with those two colors.

3. Begin by painting the darkest areas. Work your way to the lightest spots.

4. Add highlights in white and light gray. Let the underpainting dry completely. This will take two or three days.

5. Build your middle layer by scumbling opaque paint. Let the middle layer dry completely before continuing.

6. Add final glaze layers with thinned transparent paints. These layers will change the colors of the scumbled opaque paints.

Use the paper's texture to bring out the textures of your painting.

Direct Sushi

Apply the first layers with a large brush or rag. This will keep your base layer simple.

Direct painting, also called alla prima, is a bright, fresh take on oil painting. Alla prima paintings are completed in a single session.

Plan your color placement in advance. Since you'll be painting in a single session, your underlayers won't have a chance to dry. When working with wet paint, using dark colors over light will cause your paint layers to blend and appear muddy. Color the dark areas first. Then use brighter paint to mimic natural light.

1. Mix all the colors you may need onto your palette before beginning.

2. Lightly sketch your sushi. Plan which colors will go where.

3. Apply the middle tones to the canvas. Lay down basic shapes. Clean your brush between strokes and different applications of color.

4. Add highlights of color. Vary your brush strokes to represent your subject's texture. Objects in the background will have less color contrast. Objects in the foreground will need to pop.

5. Paint foreground objects with high-contrast colors and shorter strokes.

What's the Difference?

Compare the two sushi paintings. You'll notice that the direct sushi looks brighter but flatter.

Indirect painting uses layers of transparent paint over opaque. The canvas, the opaque layer, and the transparent layer can be seen in different parts of the painting. This allows light and color to interact with each other, creating depth.

Direct painting uses only opaque paint. Light bounces right off the surface of the painting. This creates a bright, reflective picture.

Seurat Dots

Far away, you see a painting with vivid color and dazzling light. Up close, you see small dots and tiny brush strokes. Each dot is a single color. The dots have come together to create an entire picture! This technique is called pointillism. French painter Georges Seurat (1859–1891) was the inventor of this technique. His most famous painting, *A Sunday on La Grande Jatte*, was created with pointillism. Borrow his technique to create this dazzling, dotted dragonfly.

Neo-What?

Georges Seurat led the Neo-Impressionistic movement (1886–1891). Painting techniques of this movement were more scientific. They explored combining separate, overlapping colors, rather than colors traditionally blended together.

1. Prime your wood panel with linseed oil. Linseed oil will preserve the wood. It acts as a barrier between the wood and the paint. Without this barrier, the paint's oil will rot the wood.

2. Sketch a rough layout of your design in pencil.

3. Mix your color palette.

4. Use round brushes or cotton swabs to create dots on your wood panel. Begin with the green background.

5. Once the background is complete, fill in the butterfly.

Think about which color blends look best together. Use similar colors to create shading. Use complementary colors to help your butterfly stand out.

Picasso's Pets

Spanish painter Pablo Picasso (1881–1973) was well known for his Blue and Rose Periods. Try copying his style by sticking with only reds and blues. Then add highlights from the opposite color palette.

Blue

1. Choose a pet whose mood matches the blue palette.

2. Use parchment paper to encourage soft brush strokes. Use painter's tape to flatten the paper and create neat edges.

3. Sketch your layout onto the paper.

4. Block the middle tones of color. Start with the largest areas. Work your way toward the smaller spaces.

5. Mix your red palette. Try for reds with a cooler tone. Use this palette to add fur texture and color.

6. Switch back to blue. Add detail to the pet's eyes and nose.

Rose

For the rose painting, start with a transparent background. Tone the entire background with a single warm color. Then find your subject by building layers of color.

1 Copy steps 1–3 from the Blue project, but pick a pet whose mood matches the rose palette.

2 Cover the paper with an underlayer of transparent Burnt Orange. Leave a small square unpainted.

3 Create the subject's form over the top of your underlayer. Build the painting with multiple layers of color from your palette.

4 Paint in fur texture and color.

5 Add detail to the pet's eyes and nose.

6 Paint color highlights to the unpainted square. Use colors from the blue palette.

Blue and Rose

Picasso's Blue Period paintings were done in shades of blue. The subjects he painted were sad and gloomy. During his Rose Period, Picasso's color choices became brighter and warmer. He often painted with pinks and reds.

Limit your palette to a basic red/blue, a secondary red/blue (such as orange/turquoise), black, and white.

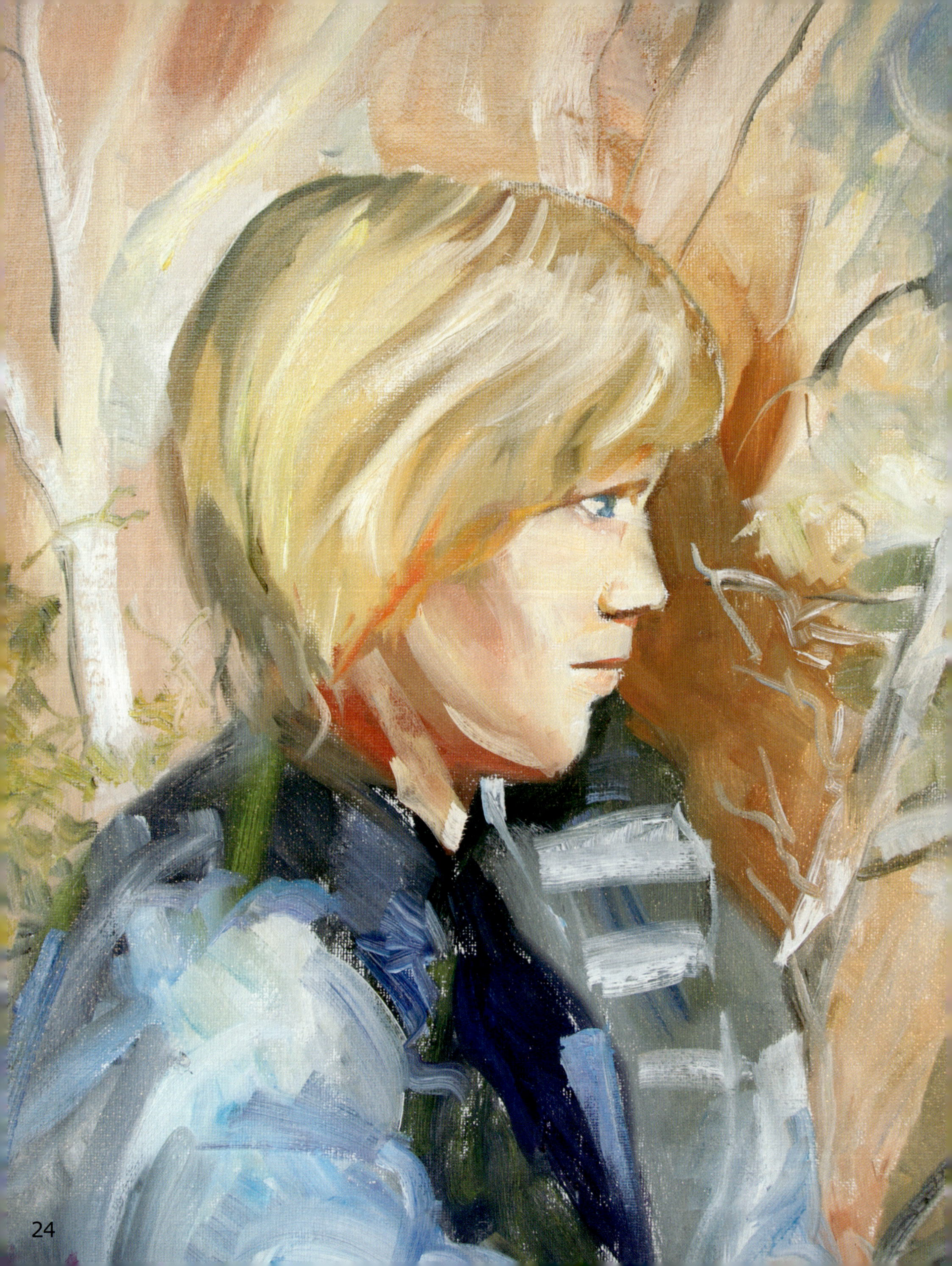

Plein Air

Why stay cooped up inside when there's plenty to paint outdoors? Gather your supplies and make your way outside! *Plein air* means "in the open air" in French. Create a portrait of your favorite person while getting some fresh air together.

1. Choose a location that will provide good light for at least an hour. Be sure your subject will be comfortable and relaxed sitting there the entire time.

2. Prepare your supplies before your subject arrives.

3. Sketch your subject in charcoal. Pay particular attention to the area around your subject, known as negative space.

4. Add shading to create a greater sense of the subject's form.

5. Working quickly, block in color and tone. A large brush will work best. Take a photograph of your subject in case you need to add more detail later.

6. Begin adding the model's base skin tone. Add base layers for the model's hair and clothing too.

continued on next page

Modern Technology

Plein air painting became popular in the late 1800s. Before, artists had to mix their own paint. This was time-consuming. But in 1867, the first premixed paint was sold. Premixed oil paints in tubes were released soon after. Around the same time, portable easels were invented. These inventions made it easy for artists to paint anywhere they wanted.

French Impressionist artists fully embraced the plein air movement. See Claude Monet and Pierre-Auguste Renoir.

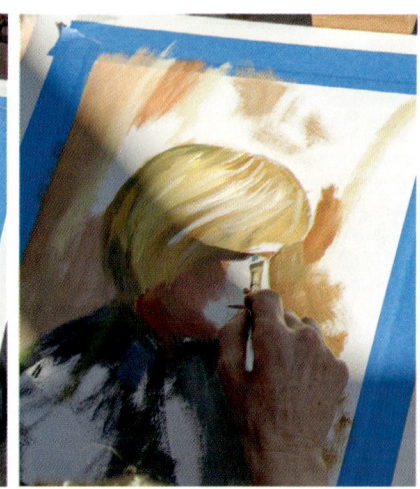

7 Continue adding to background tones.

8 Add lights/darks and warm/cool tones to the skin and hair. Pay close attention to the natural skin tones of your model and how the light affects them.

9 Continue building layers of color. Add details of the model's eyes and lips. Try to complete work on your model before the light changes. You can always finish the background later.

Aim to start painting in the late afternoon. The sunlight will be at its brightest.

26

Tips for Successful Plein Air Painting

Scout locations the day before you begin painting. Observe the location around the same time of day that you plan to paint.

When you find the perfect location, make sure it's out of the way. If it's near a home or business, get permission to paint there.

Take pictures while you paint. This will let you go back and check shadows and sunlight later.

Pack light! If you don't need an easel, don't bring it. A board to tape your canvas to works just as well, and weighs a lot less. Keep your palette small, and your brush choices even smaller.

Don't skimp on water! Bring plenty, both for your brushes and for yourself and your model.

A roll of paper towels is essential. Weigh the roll down with a PVC pipe small enough to fit inside the center tube. You can also store your brushes inside the pipe.

Be courteous! Clean up after yourself, and thank anyone who may have given you permission to paint.

Not ready for a human subject? Try painting a landscape or cityscape instead.

In the Style Of

Reinvent the salad bar with this fresh and fruity painting! Play with your food and explore the works of Italian painter Giuseppe Arcimboldo. How many features can you create to make edible art?

1. Before you begin, think about the shapes of your subject. Keep in mind the colors and textures of each piece of food. Examine the foods and how the light hits each piece. Play with the arrangement until it looks exactly how you want.

2. Prime a piece of masonite board with linseed oil.

Be sure to use hard-pressed masonite board for your painting. Other kinds are too absorbent and fall apart. Both sides of the board can be painted on.

continued on next page

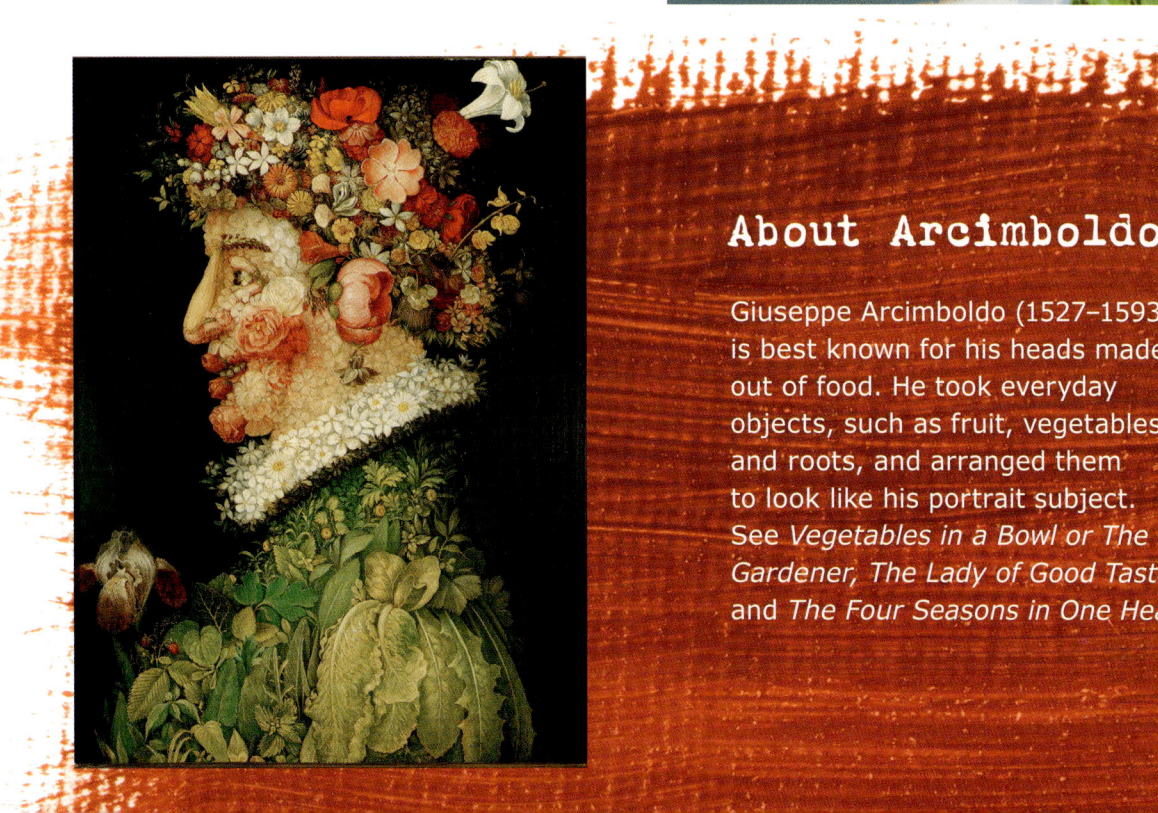

About Arcimboldo

Giuseppe Arcimboldo (1527–1593) is best known for his heads made out of food. He took everyday objects, such as fruit, vegetables, and roots, and arranged them to look like his portrait subject. See *Vegetables in a Bowl or The Gardener*, *The Lady of Good Taste*, and *The Four Seasons in One Head*.

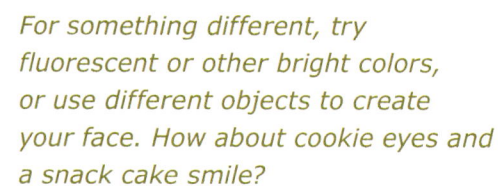

For something different, try fluorescent or other bright colors, or use different objects to create your face. How about cookie eyes and a snack cake smile?

3 Lightly sketch your composition onto the board.

4 Paint the dark background colors.

5 Paint the background shapes and colors of the fruits and vegetables.

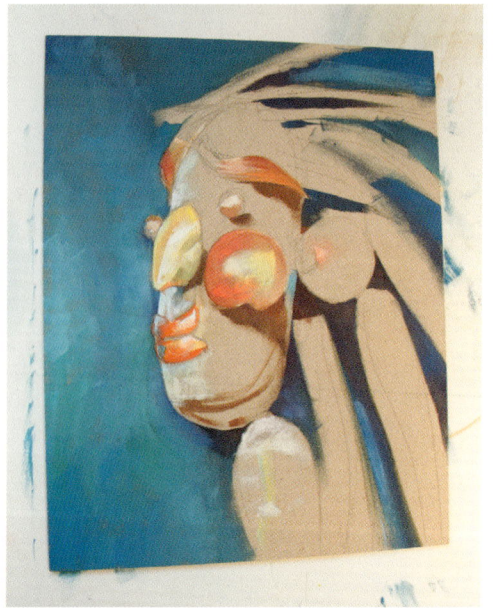

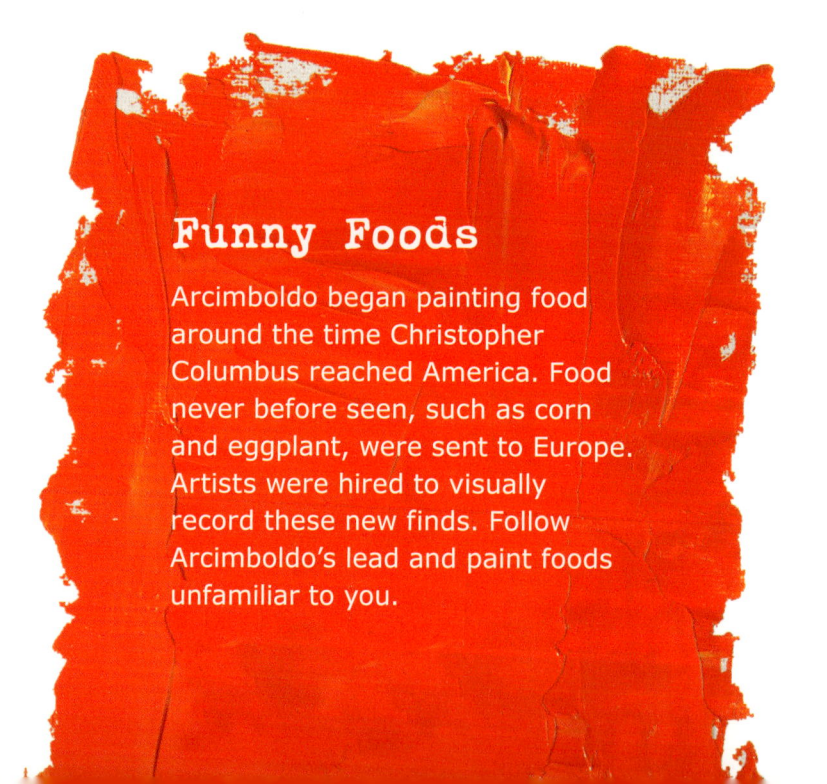

Funny Foods

Arcimboldo began painting food around the time Christopher Columbus reached America. Food never before seen, such as corn and eggplant, were sent to Europe. Artists were hired to visually record these new finds. Follow Arcimboldo's lead and paint foods unfamiliar to you.

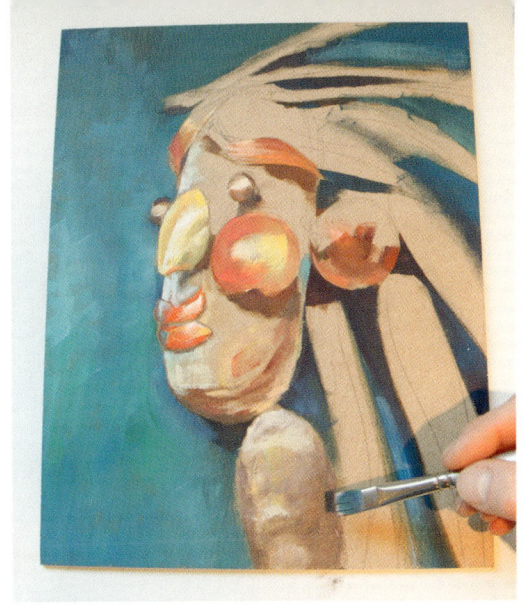

6 Add highlights and shadows to make your fruit look round. Layers of glaze will help the food pop off the page.

7 Experiment with texture. Try to give your painting the same textures as the real food. Focus on finishing each piece individually before starting the next.

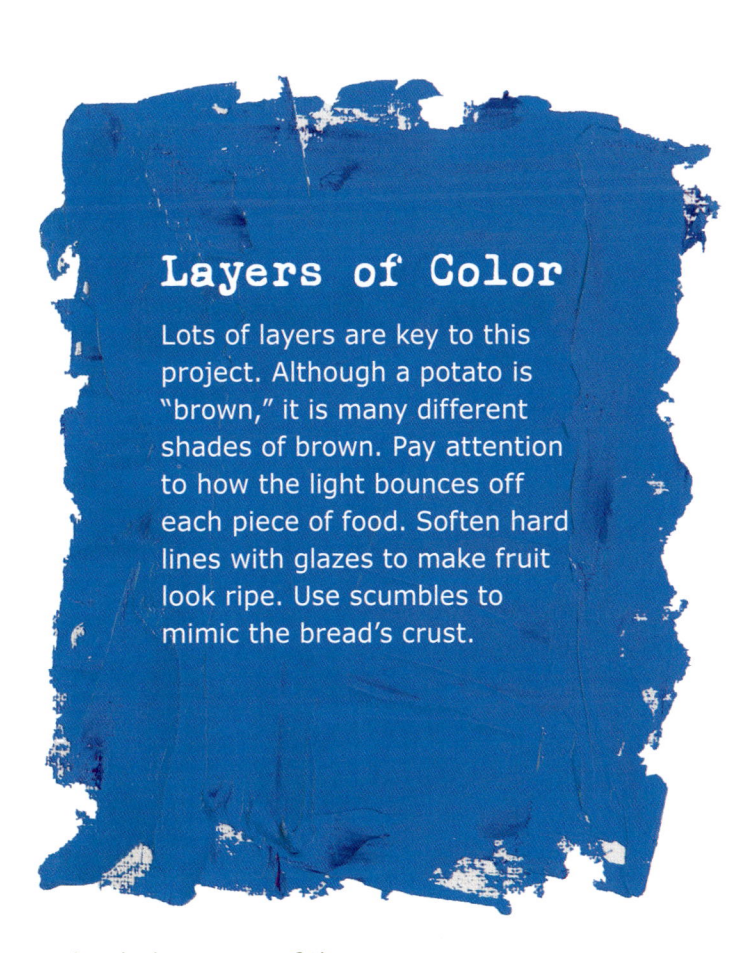

Layers of Color

Lots of layers are key to this project. Although a potato is "brown," it is many different shades of brown. Pay attention to how the light bounces off each piece of food. Soften hard lines with glazes to make fruit look ripe. Use scumbles to mimic the bread's crust.

Paint the darker areas of the background with transparent glazes. Add highlights with heavy coats of light-colored paint. The dark colors will recede, giving your painting another aspect of realism.

31

Read More

Bodden, Valerie. *History Paintings*. Brushes with Greatness. Mankato, Minn.: Creative Paperbacks, 2013.

Bolte, Mari. *Acrylics*. Paint It. North Mankato, Minn.: Capstone Press, 2014.

Wenzel, Angela. *13 Art Techniques Children Should Know*. New York: Prestel Pub. Random House, 2013.

Internet Sites

FactHound offers a safe, fun way to find Internet sites related to this book. All of the sites on FactHound have been researched by our staff.

Here's all you do:

Visit www.facthound.com

Type in this code: 9781476531106

Super-cool stuff! Check out projects, games and lots more at **www.capstonekids.com**

Author Bio

Mari Bolte is an author of children's books and a lover of art. She lives in southern Minnesota with her husband, daughter, and two wiener dogs. A degree in creative writing has taught her the value of fine writing. Parenthood has made her a purveyor of fine art, with specializations in sidewalk chalk, washable markers, and glitter glue.

Illustrator Bio

Pamela Becker, a Rhode Island School of Design alumni, enjoys the challenge of taking on projects that expand her knowledge of the world and of herself. She has traveled extensively studying mask making, mythology, and dance, which infuses her art with the patina of diversity.

JUN 23 2014